FIRST FLIGHT®

*FIRST FLIGHT® is an exciting new series
of beginning readers.
The series presents titles which include songs,
poems, adventures, mysteries, and humour
by established authors and illustrators.
FIRST FLIGHT® makes the introduction to reading fun
and satisfying for the young reader.*

*FIRST FLIGHT® is available in 4 levels
to correspond to reading development.*

Level 1 – Preschool - Grade 1
Large type, repetition of simple concepts that are perfect for reading aloud, easy vocabulary and endearing characters in short simple stories for the earliest reader.

Level 2 – Grade 1 - Grade 3
Longer sentences, higher level of vocabulary, repetition, and high-interest stories for the progressing reader.

Level 3 – Grade2 - Grade 4
Simple stories with more involved plots and a simple chapter format for the newly independent reader.

Level 4 – Grade 3 - up (First Flight Chapter Books)
More challenging level, minimal illustrations for the independent reader.

First four books in the First Flight® series

Level 1 • Fishes in the Ocean *written by* Maggee Spicer *and* Richard Thompson, *illustrated by* Barbara Hartmann

Level 2 • Jingle Bells *written and illustrated by* Maryann Kovalski

Level 3 • Andrew's Magnificent Mountain of Mittens *written by* Deanne Lee Bingham, *illustrated by* Kim LaFave

Level 4 • The Money Boot *written by* Ginny Russell, *illustrated by* John Mardon

A First Flight® Level One Reader

FISHES IN THE OCEAN

by

Maggee Spicer and Richard Thompson

illustrated by

Barbara Hartmann

Fitzhenry and Whiteside • Toronto

FIRST FLIGHT® is a registered trademark of Fitzhenry and Whiteside

First published in the United States in 1999.

Fitzhenry & Whiteside acknowledges with thanks the support of the Government of Canada through its Book Publishing Industry Development Program in the publication of this title.

Printed in Canada.

Design by Wycliffe Smith

10 9 8 7 6 5 4 3 2 1

Canadian Cataloguing in Publication Data

Spicer, Maggee
Fishes in the ocean

(A first flight level one reader)
ISBN 1-55041-395-3 (bound)   ISBN 1-55041-387-2 (pbk.)

I. Thompson, Richard, 1951-   II. Hartmann, Barbara, 1950-
III. Title. IV. Series.

PS8587.P498F57 1998   jC813'.54   C98-931760-9
PZ7.S64Fi 1998

To all my teachers:
Those whom I've met in person
and those whom I've met through
their work.

Barb

FISHES
IN THE
OCEAN

Fishes in the ocean,

Sharks in the sea,

We all go
swimming
with a

1

2

3

Eagles in the blue sky,

Seagulls by the shore,

We all go
soaring
with a

Otters doing backflips,

Frogs love to dive,

We all go
splashing
with a 3

4

5

Ducks in the barnyard,

Hens with their chicks,

We all go
waddle
with a

Sun in the blue sky,

Stars in the heavens,

We try to
reach them
with a **5**

6

7

Roosters in the morning,

Owls when it's late,

We
stretch
and **yawn**
with a **6**

7

8

19

Snakes in a wriggle,

Ants in a line,

We all go
marching
with a

Dog in the doghouse,

Pigs in the pen,

We all have

a **rest**

with an

8

9

10

10

9

8

24

Getting kind of late!

Glad to be alive

I love you!

This book is done...